For Mum.
T.T.F.N.

Published exclusively for J Sainsbury plc
Stamford Street London SE1 9LL
by Walker Books Ltd
87 Vauxhall Walk London SE11 5HJ

First printed 1991
Reprinted 1992

© 1991 Nick Butterworth

ISBN 0-7445-1672-2

MY GRANDMA IS
WONDERFUL

Nick Butterworth

SAINSBURY · WALKER BOOKS

My grandma is wonderful.

She always buys
the biggest ice-creams…

and she never, ever loses
at noughts and crosses…

and she knows
all about nature…

and she's brilliant at
untying knots…

and she's always on your side
when things go wrong…

and she makes the most fantastic clothes…

and when you're ill,
she can make you forget
that you don't feel well…

and she can scream
really loudly...

and she has
marvellous hearing...

and no matter where you are,
she always has what you need
in her handbag.

It's great to have
a grandma like mine.

She's wonderful!